Birthday Mice!

Birthday Mice!

BY BETHANY ROBERTS

ILLUSTRATED BY DOUG CUSHMAN

Green Light Readers

HOUGHTON MIFFLIN HARCOURT

Boston   New York

www.hmhco.com

The Library of Congress has cataloged the hardcover edition as follows:
Roberts, Bethany.
Birthday mice!/by Bethany Roberts; illustrated by Doug Cushman
p. cm.
Summary: A little mouse's very lively birthday party has the cowboy theme
he hoped for.
[1. Birthdays—Fiction. 2. Parties—Fiction. 3. Cowboys—Fiction. 4. Mice—
Fiction. 5. Animals—Fiction. 6. Stories in rhyme.] I. Cushman, Doug, ill.
II. Title.
PZ8.3.R5295 Bi2002
[E] 21
2001047594

ISBN: 978-0-544-45606-8 GLR paperback
ISBN: 978-0-544-45605-1 GLR paper over board

Manufactured in China
SCP 10 9 8 7 6 5 4 3 2 1

4500512346

*Happy birthday, Cowboy Adam
and Cowboy Zach!*
—B.R.

*To Jennifer Greene, who waited
ages for this birthday party*
—D.C.

Birthday mice
get ready for a party.

One little mouse
is two, two, two!

Balloons, balloons,
blow them up.

Red, yellow,
and blue, blue, blue!

Yippee-yi-yo!
Yippee-yi-yay!

A birthday cowboy.
Clippity-clop!

Howdy, cowboy!

Whoa! Watch out!

Oh, no!

POP! POP! POP!

The guests are coming.
Party time!

Here come the squirrels,
the rabbits too.

Cowboy boots that
stomp, stomp, stomp!

The chipmunks brings
a rope lasso.

Skunk gives spurs
that jingle, jangle.

Perfect for a
buckaroo!

Now let's play!
Sing cowboy songs!

Cowboy dancing,
do-si-do!

Wrangler whoops
and cowhand hollers!

Swing your partner
round and . . .

. . . OH!

The cake is smashed,
balloons are popped.

The party is
a mess, mess, mess!

Blow more balloons! And for the cake—
cowboy vittles. Yes, yes, yes!

Blow out the candles!
Wish, wish, wish!

I wish . . .
for a horse.

A horse?
Of course!

But how?
But how?

Magic, presto!
Zappity-zorse!

Yippee-yi-yo!
Yippee-yi-yay!
A horse for a mouse
to gallop away!

RAVES FOR JAMES PATTERSON AND HIS BRILLIANT AND BELOVED HERO ALEX CROSS

"IF THERE REALLY WERE HUMAN SUPERHEROES, ALEX CROSS WOULD BE AT THE HEAD OF THE CLASS."
—*New York Times*

"CROSS IS ONE OF THE BEST AND MOST LIKABLE CHARACTERS IN THE MODERN THRILLER GENRE."
—*San Francisco Examiner*

"IN ALEX CROSS, WHO HAPPENS TO BE BLACK, THE EDGAR AWARD WINNER HAS CREATED A MOST COMPELLING HERO…He's the kind of multilayered character that makes any plot twist seem believable."
—*People*

"THERE ARE NO FASTER READS THAN PATTERSON'S ALEX CROSS BOOKS."
—*Denver Rocky Mountain News*

"WHEN IT COMES TO CONSTRUCTING A HARROWING PLOT, AUTHOR JAMES PATTERSON CAN TURN A SCREW ALL RIGHT."
—*New York Daily News*

"THE MAN IS A MASTER OF HIS GENRE. We fans all have one wish for him: Write even faster."
—Larry King, *USA Today*

"PATTERSON KNOWS WHERE OUR DEEPEST FEARS ARE BURIED…THERE'S NO STOPPING HIS IMAGINATION."
—*New York Times Book Review*

"PATTERSON HAS A UNIQUE GIFT FOR MAKING THE READER FEEL CROSS'S JOYS AND PAINS."
—*San Francisco Examiner*

"ANYONE READING AN ALEX CROSS NOVEL CAN'T HELP BUT WANT MORE OF HIM."
—*Midwest Book Review*